GRANDDADDY'S TURN

GRANDDADDY'S TURN

A Journey to the Ballot Box

Michael S. Bandy and Eric Stein

illustrated by James E. Ransome

CANDLEWICK PRESS

Where we lived, I didn't need an alarm clock.

I woke up to the *cock-a-doodle-doo* of my pet rooster and the *chucka, chucka, chucka* of my granddaddy's tractor.

"Hurry up, boy," he would shout.

"I'm coming, Granddaddy," I'd say.

"We got work to do," my granddaddy would say. "Hard work will keep you out of trouble."

I guess he figured I was going to get in a whole passel of trouble, because he sure gave me lots of chores.

We fed the animals. We milked the cows. And we worked in the fields.

My granddaddy was a big, strong man who always said he "didn't take nothing off nobody." He could do anything—plow fields, chop wood, and dig fence posts, all without breaking a sweat.

Not like me! Sometimes when I did my chores, I made so much sweat, it was like I was raining.

We worked together a lot. But we played a lot, too. We really loved to go fishing.

Sometimes I would complain when I didn't get a bite right away, but my granddaddy always said, "Patience, son, patience."

One morning while we were eating breakfast, my grandmother brought out a surprise for my granddaddy. She had cleaned and ironed his suit. I didn't understand that, since he only wore his suit to church—and it wasn't a church day.

"It's our time, and you got to look your best!" my grandma said.

My granddaddy was so excited, he leaped up from the table and gave her a big hug.

"What's going on, Granddaddy?" I asked.

"You'll see," he said with a big, beaming smile.

I didn't like neckties too much, but since my granddaddy was wearing one, I guess I was, too.

"Y'all be careful, now," my grandma said. "And don't forget to take pictures," she said as she handed my granddaddy the camera.

We walked and walked—it seemed like a hundred miles. I asked my granddaddy where we were going again.

"Patience, son, patience," he reminded me with a smile.

Oh, boy! I thought. *We must be going to the county fair.* I walked faster. I couldn't wait to get there. I could almost hear the music and smell the barbecue.

"Where are all the rides and animals?" I asked my granddaddy.

He laughed and said, "What are you talking about, son?"

"I thought we were going to the county fair," I said.

"Take a look around," my granddaddy said. "This is better than any old fair."

Then I saw the VOTE HERE sign and shouted to my granddaddy, "Are you voting today?"

"Yes, I am," my granddaddy proudly replied.

Nobody in my family had ever voted before. Where we lived, some people were allowed to vote and some people were not. I never knew anyone who had voted before.

But I heard my teacher say that some new laws had changed all that.

I hoped that was true, because I didn't want us to get in trouble.

It felt like we were standing in line forever, and every time we seemed to get a little closer, someone would cut in line in front of us. That's just how things worked where we lived.

It didn't seem to bother my granddaddy, though. He said, "Patience, son. Takes patience to get what you've got coming to you!"

When we finally got to the front of the line, my granddaddy proudly signed a paper and was handed a ballot.

He clutched the ballot to his chest and said, "Son, this is the happiest day of my life."

I took the camera from him and said, "Smile, Granddaddy."

"Now, come on—let's go vote," he said.

But before we could even walk to the voting booth, a deputy stopped us and asked my granddaddy, "What are you doing, Uncle?"

Where we lived, if the white folks didn't know your name, they usually called you either Uncle or George—or Auntie if you were a lady.

"I'm voting today, sir," my granddaddy replied.

The deputy got out a big, thick book and slammed it on the table. He opened it to a page with words that looked longer than crawfish.

"Can you read this, Uncle?" the deputy asked.

My granddaddy just stared at the pages and shook his head. "No, sir, I can't," he replied.

The deputy slammed the book shut, saying, "Well, Uncle, if you can't read this, then you can't vote." He tore up my granddaddy's ballot and threw it on the ground.

I was pretty sure that man wasn't playing by the rules, but he was in charge. I could see my granddaddy was mad.

As we headed back down the road toward home, my granddaddy
didn't say a word. But I saw something I'd never seen before—my big,
strong granddaddy had tears in his eyes.

"Don't worry, Granddaddy. I'll vote for you one day," I said to him.

Granddaddy passed away before he ever got a chance to vote.

I never forgot that day he tried to vote. My granddaddy was so mad, he might've lost his temper. But he knew better than me how important that day was. Even though it wasn't his time to vote that day, he looked to the future.

When I went to vote for the first time, I remembered what my granddaddy always said: "Patience, son, patience." He was right. The day finally came. And I knew that—just like my granddaddy—I would never take it for granted.

With his picture in my hand, I put my ballot in the box, smiled, and said to myself, *Now it's Granddaddy's turn.*

Thanks to Spencer Humphrey, Ed Labowitz, Nicole Raymond,
Karen Lotz, and Congressman John Lewis —M. S. B.

For my uncle, Phil Stein —E. S.

Thank you to the generation that walked, rode, protested, sat in,
and opened all the doors for my generation —J. E. R.

★ ★ ★

In the 1950s and 1960s, the civil rights movement helped dismantle the walls of racial segregation in the United States brick by brick—from interstate transportation to access to education to the desegregation of public accommodations and housing.

The last vestige of resistance in this struggle was voting rights. The pro-segregation establishment clearly understood the power of the vote. The concept of one person, one vote has always been the key to significant political and social change—a change that segregationists were not going to concede without a fight.

Politically sanctioned nullification of voter rights was commonplace in Alabama and many other southern states. African-American citizens were subject to various unethical methods of voter suppression, including poll taxes and birth-record challenges. Perhaps the worst of these tactics were the so-called literacy tests.

These tests were usually administered by the polling officials toward any individual who was considered "undesirable." The potential voter was handed a booklet or pamphlet, which often consisted of a difficult Elizabethan text or complex legal language. The voter was asked to read the document aloud and to explain in detail to the polling official what the passages meant. If the explanation was not deemed up to par, the voter was dismissed and not allowed to vote.

Through these tactics, thousands of individuals were denied their constitutional right to vote; many were also harassed or hurt, and some were even killed. Fortunately, these practices were ultimately stopped with the passage of the 1965 Voting Rights Act, landmark legislation signed into law by President Lyndon B. Johnson.